Jimmy just has to lay hands on a Tottenham Hotspur scout. Otherwise Georgie and Ginger are going to defect. And the new Riverside U-10s will sink before they swim.

Chippy has an idea (well he would, wouldn't he?): ask Brains O'Mahony. And it turns out Brains O'Mahony *can* help. But he wants Jimmy to do a favour for a friend of his. It involves Da. Which, given how things are between Jimmy and Da most of the time, could be more than a bit tricky …

Peter Regan

RIVERSIDE
Scout!

Illustrated by Terry Myler

THE CHILDREN'S PRESS

For

Jenna and Jackson Heinrichs

First published 2000 by
The Children's Press
an imprint of Anvil Books
45 Palmerston Road, Dublin 6

3 5 6 4 2

© Text Peter Regan
© Illustrations Terry Myler

ISBN 1 901737 22 5

Typeset by Computertype Limited
Printed by Colour Books Limited

Contents

1 Dynamo Rouge Bows Out

Hi, it's me, Jimmy Quinn. My Dynamo Rouge U-10 team has been taken over by Riverside Boys, lock, stock and barrel. They'll be playing for Mr Glynn and Harry Hennessy in future. Still, Flintstone and me have been asked to stay on and give a hand with the team. More about that later.

A week before the takeover I decided to field my Dynamo Rouge team one last time. The match was against Southern Cross Cosmos, as we wanted to make the occasion a day out. See, the Southern Cross area is right next to the countryside and the Little Sugarloaf Mountain. Being late August we'd go early, have a picnic, a bit of adventure, leave the match until evening.

There was also another reason for playing Cosmos. I intended asking Sean Mulligan, their centre-half, to sign for Riverside's new U-10 team. I'd pop the question to him afterwards. Sean Mulligan is a class centre-half, the best in Bray for his age.

On the day, the sun was splitting the sky all across the Little Sugarloaf as far as Bray Head. The sky was so blue, it resembled the Pacific Ocean turned upside down.

After getting off the bus we went through one of the housing estates, The locals stared at us as if we'd just landed from Mars. We were strung out all over the place. A few were on the path, a few on the road, more on the knee-high red-brick walls that fronted the gardens in the housing estate.

What's more, Baby Joe McCann was out front walking backwards with a car mirror in his hand. Most of us were gobbling crisps. Flintstone was at the back of the cavalcade, no better than a camel, loaded with football gear.

Ignoring any prying eyes that might be watching the Sultans of Football pass by, we climbed over a wall into the countryside. There was nothing but green fields and woods close to the shoulder of the Little Sugarloaf. There were no roads, no houses, no nothing. It was exactly like Gypsy Walshe described it – 'The Wild West'.

'We ain't goin' to walk all the way, are we?' moaned Nobby Roche.

'What do you think?' I barked back. 'Course we are! We're goin' to the top. But you need only go halfway. We'll have what's called Base Camp One there.'

'Like on Mount Everest?'

'Yeah, just like Mount Everest. You and Flintstone can wait there and look after the football gear.'

Flintstone objected. On account of being a regular mountain goat he wanted to go to the top of the Little Sugarloaf. But I bribed him with a mix of confiscated crisps and Mars Bars. That made him happy enough to stay at Base Camp with Nobby and look after the football kit while we were gone.

When we got near the woods on the slope of the Sugarloaf, I called a temporary halt. I gave a short speech:

'Far away is Mount Everest, a hundred times the size of the Little Sugarloaf. Where we stand today there is no blinding snow, no icy ravines, none of the dangers of Mount Everest. But, the Little Sugarloaf is still a mountain. In the next half hour we'll conquer its peak. In doing so, those of you who'll be playing for Riverside will be strengthened as a team, capable of taking on the world and winning all before you.'

I thought I had touched the right chord. At least until some smart alec opened his mouth.

'We'll be too nackered. We won't be able to beat anyone. Not Southern Cross Cosmos anyway.'

That had to be that drip John Nolan. He was one of the players, along with Sean Dodd and Niall Cooper, who wouldn't be kept on by Riverside. Whatever about the other two, I'd be glad to see the back of John Nolan. What a mouth!

When we got to the top, nackered or not, I could sense the spirit of the mountain spreading to the players. We were soaring above the earth. Bray sprawled below us, people so small they almost didn't exist. If ever there was a moment for inspiration, this was it. That's until some thick broke the spell: 'There's smoke down there.'

And there was.

It came from the copse of trees nearest the summit of the Little Sugarloaf.

'Smoke signals. Must be Indians,' said Pee Wee Flood.

'Don't be daft,' shrugged Catho. 'No way is it Indians.'

And neither was it Indians.

Catho had put his finger on it. See, Catho is smart. He has to be, especially on account of being able to play the cello. Some people have plenty of brains. Catho is one of them. Everything he says makes sense. That's why people listen to him.

Tootsie Devlin and Gypsy Walshe were missing! They must have sneaked off during the climb and gone to the wood. Very probably they were responsible for the smoke, meaning a box of matches had got out of control.

We ran down the Little Sugarloaf in double-quick time, made straight for the wood.

We weren't long in finding the two lads. They were beating the smouldering under-growth with light branches, trying to put the fire out.

'How'd it happen?' I roared.

'It was Gypsy. He was messin'. Said we'd start a fire.'

'I did not!'

We all grabbed bits of branches – the three girls Gemma Murphy, Regina Moore and Emma Short were first off the mark – and thumped the living daylights out of the undergrowth.

Talking of Emma, the game against Cosmos was to be her last trip with us. Her mother wouldn't let her play for the team any more. Said she didn't want Emma picking up the rough accent most of us had. What she meant was her daughter was beginning to sound like the oul' ones who sell fish and vegetables in Moore Street in Dublin.

It was nice and peaceful for Flintstone and Nobby back at Base Camp One, basking in the sunshine, Flintstone in a pair of Boston Celtic tracksuit bottoms, Nobby in a pair of football shorts. It was all right for them. The sweat fairly rolled off us. What's more, we got covered in black soot from the smoke.

It didn't stay all right for Flintstone and

Nobby for very long. Some firemen rolled up in a fire-engine.

Nobby knew what to say. Nothing.

But Flintstone didn't. He got us into a right mess of trouble.

'They're up there,' he said

'Who?'

'Our mates. Where the smoke is.'

The firemen took off on Shanks's mare, straight to the wood. They gave us a blasting.

Looking back, it was as well they arrived, because they put an end to the smouldering.

'It's the heat from the sun,' I said. 'Combustion it's called.'

'That so?'

'Internal combustion,' added Tootsie.

'Internal, is it?'

'Yeah. Maybe it's eternal though.'

That put an end to the small talk. Luckily, the firemen didn't ask for our names, or say they'd get the law. Strangely, apart from the fire, I think they took a liking to us.

On the way down to Base Camp One, I made Gypsy Walshe empty his pockets. Three full boxes of matches fell out. I lit every last one in front of him. He tried to make up an excuse, that some oul' wan sent him on a message to the shops and he forgot to give the matches to her. We all knew he was in the wrong – and said so.

If Mad Victor hadn't gone out of our lives to Birmingham he would have got it all on video-tape, the view from the top of the Little Sugarloaf, the firemen, the smoke, the lot. Even me giving out to Gypsy Walshe like I was John Wayne.

We missed the brother, Mad Henry, too, especially at outside-right. The only solution was to move Regina Moore into his place. Football-wise she's a better player, only she hasn't his strength, or heart. See, Mad Henry is full of heart. He never gives up.

On account of giving out to Gypsy Walshe I could sense the kids regarded me with a lot more respect – a sense that they knew I was in charge and wasn't to be messed about. It's important for managers not to be messed about, especially by nine and ten-year-olds. For me, it made the trip to the Little Sugarloaf all the more worthwhile.

By the time we got to the Southern Cross Cosmos pitch we only had an hour to kill. We pestered the oul' wans to let us into their homes to have a wash. Most of us were so black with soot that only the whites of our eyes showed. But none of the oul' wans allowed us in, even Catho. And he's a real gentleman. He speaks posher than anyone I've ever met.

You'd think we'd be worn out after all the excitement on the Little Sugarloaf, but we had a good half-hour doss on the pitch. I think some of the locals thought we were travellers, waiting for the caravans to arrive. When we put on our football gear they knew different.

I wasn't half glad to see Sean Mulligan tog out for Cosmos. I was afraid he might have gone off somewhere for the summer. But I needn't have worried. He was out there on the pitch, doing what he does best, playing football.

Soon as the match was over (we won 1-3) I had a word with him in private.

'Like to play for Riverside Boys this season?'

'Is that the team?'

'No, there's a few of this lot won't make it.'

'Like who?'

'Like John Nolan, like Niall Cooper, like Nick Reilly, that kind of player,'

'What about the girls?'

'Only two. We've a few new players coming in.'

'Anyone I know?'

'Georgie O'Connor and Ginger Mullin.'

'They play for Ardmore.'

'Not any more. They've signed for Riverside … on account of Mr Glynn.'

'Why?'

'Because he's going to be the manager. Him and Harry Hennessy.'

'Who's that Chinese fella?'

'Catho. He's not Chinese. He's from Singapore.'

I'd only found out that lately. We'd always thought he was Chinese, but not any more.

'He's a good player. With the likes of him on your team I just might sign. I'll think about it.'

'Give us your address. I'll get Mr Glynn to have a chat with you.'

He gave me his address.

Soon as he did, I had a gut feeling he'd sign for Riverside Boys.

Our trip to the Little Sugarloaf proved to be worthwhile for all.

Players of Sean Mulligan's quality aren't easily found.

But he'd been found now. What's more, he'd start the season in a Riverside jersey.

2 Demotion!

Mr Glynn wasn't long in getting my ex-team into a league – the North Wicklow Schoolboy League. At least it was a proper league, affiliated to the SFAI (Schoolboy Football Association of Ireland).

When Chippy, Flintstone, Mad Victor and the rest of us first played for Riverside, we played in a non-affiliated league for a bit.

It was an experience. Murder actually. No sooner were we in than they wanted us out. We were too good for them, see. As soon as we started winning, the oul' lads on the committee started saying we were all over-age. Only they couldn't prove it. No one could. Because we weren't over-age. We didn't even look it. Except maybe Mad Victor who was pretty hefty. But the committee wouldn't let up. Said we were only a shower of bangers from Bray.

The chairman said it.

The secretary said it.

The treasurer said it.

They all said it.

The chairman said it again. He was a real pain in the neck. You could hear the hate in his voice, even if he did speak with a posh accent. He ran a team in the league. We were due to play them in a shield final a few weeks later. On form, we were sure to win.

On D-Day we were down 3-0 at half-time. They'd built a pitch with a bit of a slope so they could get a head start. And as they had won the toss – they hadn't got where they were by losing tosses – they did just that. But we killed them in the second half and won 3-5.

I don't know which was best. Winning the shield or seeing the look on the chairman's face. It would have turned vinegar sour.

That was the old days, sadly all gone now. But not for Chippy, Flintstone and me. Chippy would be playing for a new Riverside Youth team in the Dublin Schoolboys League. They wouldn't be pitched against the top teams in Dublin. They were down to play in the 'C' section, nothing over-lofty, probably about all they'd be able to handle. Almost at the last minute, Chippy had given up the idea of playing junior football in the Wicklow League and signed for Mr Glynn's new Youth team. Pity he hadn't made his mind up a few weeks earlier; we could have kept our Riverside U-14 team together. Pity, but at least Chippy would still be a Riverside player, and he wouldn't run the risk of picking up a bad injury at junior level. Flintstone and I weren't playing any more but due to my success as manager of Dynamo Rouge, I'd been assigned to Riverside's new U-10 team, but not as manager. My main job was to make sure the players knew all the arrangements for match days. I'd be nothing more than a glorified messenger-boy, a big drop in rank.

I had to swallow my pride. It wasn't easy. How could it be? Imagine Alex Ferguson having the team taken away from him? Made go around on a bicycle, knocking on players' doors, raving on about last-minute changes and cock-ups? Humiliation is the word; that's how it was for me.

Not that the bicycle belonged to me; it belonged to Harry Hennessy. He used it when lapping the players around the Park during training, when Flintstone didn't take charge. *He* didn't need a bike. He'd usually lose the run of himself and end up miles ahead, lapping them a few times, no bother.

Lately, since Harry and Arthur Guinness have fallen out, he's taken to going for a spin on the bike around Bray. The exercise has had a good effect on his health. He doesn't look as puffed in the face. His weight is down – down half a notch on his belt. But with all the huff and puff he is still Harry – a very fat Harry at that.

Only consolation for me. Youth and U-10 fixtures were both set for Sundays, maybe meaning when Mr Glynn would be away with the Youth team he'd leave Harry Hennessy in charge, with me as assistant manager. I had the edge on Harry and I'd leave my mark once Mr Glynn wasn't around. Harry would be manager in name: I'd run the show. I'd edge in gradually. At worst, I'd be equal joint manager.

What surprised me most about the new U-10 team was the attitude of Georgie

O'Connor and Ginger Mullin. They proved to be real Riverside true-blues. Apart from Sean Mulligan or Catho, if there was a ready-made captain it was between the two of them.

'We don't mind which of us is captain, Mr Glynn. Do as you please.'

Which he did by making the two lads draw lots, meaning he held two matches in his hand. Whoever drew the longer one would be captain, the short one vice-captain. Georgie drew the longer one.

'Me brother Jamesie was captain of River-

side once,' he stated afterwards.

'One of the best captains going,' remembered Mr Glynn, happy with the way events had turned out.

And a good captain is important. Players look up to a good captain. What's more, good captains lead by example. They make ordinary players rise above themselves, make them play with pride and spirit.

Georgie and Ginger had plenty of pride and spirit. Wild horses wouldn't have drawn them away from Ardmore, but Riverside did. You see, they had the club in their blood.

Shay Lynch, their ex-manager at Ardmore wasn't feeling too good about them leaving. He was gutted. Georgie and Ginger were probably the two best midfielders in the entire North Wicklow League. They'd instill plenty of fighting spirit into our new U-10 team. And it would be needed! Ardmore, Wolfe Tone, Newtown, Kilcoole, Greystones (not Shamrock Boys), Ashford, Valeview and a powerhouse of a team from Wicklow town were all lined up as opponents.

Talking of Wicklow, Georgie told us a good

one about when his brother Jamesie played against Wicklow years ago.

'What's your name?' Mr Glynn had asked this giant of a Wicklow U-12.

'Billy Byrne.'

'What age are you?'

'Ten and a half.'

'Where do you live?'

'The Market Square, Wicklow town.'

Georgie told us quite a few Billy Byrnes played for Wicklow over the years. And they all lived on the Market Square.

'How's that, Georgie?'

'Ever been to Wicklow town?'

'A few times.'

'Ever see the statue on the top of the town?'

'The one from 1798 of the lad with the pike in his hand?'

'The very one.'

'Has the statue got something to do with Billy Byrne?'

'The statue *is* Billy Byrne, mate.'

Now that Georgie had warned us, we'd watch out for Billy Byrne.

Especially if he had his pike with him.

3 Word from Mad Victor

On and off I was wondering how Mad Victor and Henry were doing in Birmingham. Then one sunny September day, a letter arrived in the post from England. Victor's scrawly writing was on the envelope.

Dear Jimmy,

Tell the lads I'm asking for them.

How's Chippy getting on? Is he still nuts on playing men's football?

Henry's asking for all his mates. He's wondering how the U-10s are getting on. What league are they in? Did you get any new players? Who took Henry's place?

Henry's not playing football over here. To cheer himself up, he goes to a big club every Saturday and Sunday – an Irish Club they call it. He does Irish dancing there. Says it reminds him of home. Lucky for him.

Birmingham is full of foreigners. You can't turn a corner, there's a foreigner. I know it's England, but you'd think all the races in the world lived here.

Terry's been very good to us. So have his relatives. He has plenty of them – a whole streetful.

The bit we've seen of Birmingham we don't like. Apart from a few places, everywhere we've been is full of factories and waste ground. There's plenty of high-rise flats too.

It's very dear into football matches. There's two big teams, Aston Villa and Birmingham. Birmingham wear blue and play at St Andrew's. I've seen them play twice.

I'm going to school over here. So is Henry. We hate it. If you don't go to school you can be lifted by the police. It's not safe to walk around once school is on. It's not safe to walk around at any time, far as I can see.

They call themselves 'Brums' over here, meaning that's a name they use to explain they're from Birmingham.

I don't think me and Henry'll ever be Brums.

Do us a favour? Check and see if me

uncles still have the house. Write back soon and let me know. If they're still there me and Henry might come home. We don't like it here, not any more.

Are your sisters still away?

If so, could we stay with you for a while?

If they're back, do me a favour. Give them hassle, so they get fed-up and want to leave. Then me and Henry could have their room and stay until we get fixed up elsewhere!

Like I said, we hate it here. We're thinking of coming home once we save the fare.

Hope to see you soon.

Tell all the gang I was askin' for them.

Tell Mr Glynn and Harry Hennessy too.

Your mate,
Victor

PS. How's Mrs O'Leary? Is she dead yet?

The letter wasn't exactly well-penned. Having writing skills myself I would have polished it up a bit, made it more presentable. And the spelling was dire (I've corrected it). But whatever about the way it was written, Victor certainly got the message across – he hated Birmingham. It wouldn't be long before he and Henry would be beating my door down looking for somewhere to stay.

Talking of Victor and his letter, my own writing career as the 'phantom' writer of graffiti on walls came to a sudden end.

See, we have a weird cop in Bray. He spends a lot of time near the station. Not the police station, the Bray Dart station, drinking cups of tea with the staff. We have a name for him: 'Hot Pursuit'. See, he's connected by walkie-talkie to Bray Garda station. Sometimes they ring him if there's a spot of bother nearby. He always answers by saying, 'I'm in hot pursuit.' He doesn't have a squad-car, or a motor-bike, just his two legs.

Well, one Saturday night, I was in a lane-way working on a masterpiece of graffiti when Hot Pursuit came across me unawares.

'Wha' ye doin' there, boyo?'

'Trying to scrub this graffiti off the wall.'

'Where's yer scrubbin' brush, boyo?'

'Must have fallen outa me hand with the fright you gave me.'

'Well, let's see if I can find it for ye.'

Hot Pursuit shone his torch on the pitch-black ground, pretending to be looking for the scrubbing brush, meaning the paint spray I was using on the wall.

'Don't see it here, boyo. Maybe it's gone with the fairies.'

Hot Pursuit is from Connemara. He likes to talk about fairies and leprechauns to the likes of us, thinking he's broadening our minds, making us better people. The really weird thing about him is that if he ever catches us doing something wrong he never tells us we're breaking the law; just goes on about how we'll have bad luck, that we won't grow any more, that we'll become stunted wonders: 'Stunted wonders, boyo.'

Well, this time I hit it lucky with Hot Pursuit. I'd heard him coming in the nick of time and threw the paint spray over the far side of the wall.

In the end, he let me go. But the incident left its mark. I wouldn't be into graffiti any more. I was now on Hot Pursuit's list of prime suspects. No, the graffiti business was a lost cause. I'd give it up, pronto.

See, Hot Pursuit has this thing about him. He can appear out of nowhere.

Mind you, he can disappear just as quickly.

Hot Pursuit: King of the Crafty Cops.

Getting back to Victor's letter from Birmingham, how could he expect me to get rid of my sisters? That was daft. If I drove them out they could end up with nowhere to live. Fancy going up the town some night and finding them huddled in a shop doorway, maybe sleeping in a giant-sized cardboard box! I couldn't do that, not to my sisters. After all, they're family. But I didn't want to depress Victor any more. Maybe I'd write and let on I was trying to get rid of them. Make up a few tall tales of how I was trying my hardest to get them out of the house so as he and Henry could come and stay.

So I wrote back to Victor and told him a pack of lies. I told him I was scaring my sisters witless but that there was no sign of them moving – not yet. The only bit of truth I told him was that I'd been around to his uncles' council house but they no longer lived there. The new people hadn't a clue where they'd gone to. They'd never heard of Victor's uncles, much less met them.

They did tell me one thing:

'When we moved in we had to hire two skips to get rid of all the junk. There was nothing but empty beer cans and loads of scrap. Bad enough if the stuff was only out at the back. But it was everywhere, under tables, on chairs, even under the beds. It was hard work clearing the place. We're only getting it back into shape now.'

I didn't wait to hear any more. I was half afraid they'd ask me into the house to help tidy-up. Soon as they stopped talking I scarpered down the road as quick as I could.

A week later I received another letter from Birmingham. There were two sheets of paper inside the envelope. One was from Victor, the other from Henry. They were both frantic; they couldn't wait to come home. They wanted to know how much longer it would take me to get rid of my sisters. I was their only hope.

Only hope?

What a mess!

All of a sudden I had a problem I couldn't get rid of.

4 Showdown with Chippy

Chippy's coming back to play for Riverside's Youth team meant he had a change of heart towards the rest of us: meaning he wanted to know us again. He wanted to be part of the gang once more; go places with us, share a laugh, that kind of caper. As we were all back at school we couldn't avoid him, especially as most of us were in the same class. But he began to go out of his way to be extra friendly. He even wanted to give me and Flintstone a hand to train the new team.

The new arrangement suited Mr Glynn fine. It meant he could show up at training for a few minutes, give a team talk, say who'd be playing at the weekend, and go home.

Harry Hennessy's attitude was something similar. He tagged along on the bike for the lapping and sprints. After that he'd go off, satisfied he'd lost another few pounds in weight. He'd gone on a diet lately, but it didn't last long. Hunger is a terrible thing as it didn't take Harry long to find out.

Looking back on the start of the season, the player who impressed me most was Sean Mulligan, our new signing from Southern Cross Cosmos. He'd improved our defence beyond recognition but I knew there would no point in mentioning the fact to Georgie and Ginger. As far as they were concerned they were Number One.

By the time we'd played our third match in the league Chippy had got well in with the players. He was especially friendly with Georgie and Ginger. They idolised him. He only had to produce a ball and juggle it with his feet, do a few tricks, and they'd be all over him as if he was Ronaldo. At first, we just grinned and put up with it. But in the end my shoulders began to droop.

To be fair, the kids weren't interested in just Chippy performing his bag of tricks; they wanted Flintstone and me to do the same. They wanted to see us juggle the ball with our feet a bit, tip it off our heads.

I got to fourteen with the juggling.

Flintstone got to six.

Chippy got to forever.

'Flintstone, you're brutal!'

Ginger Mullin said it.

'Jimmy, you're not much better!'

This time it was Georgie.

All of a sudden, I wished Georgie and Ginger would go back to Ardmore. But now that Chippy was on the scene piebald horses wouldn't have driven them away.

Chippy had other skills too. There were that many that he set aside twenty minutes for skill training. Whenever that happened, Flintstone and I made up an excuse and hid for the

duration. It wouldn't have been so bad if there had been only one ball but Chippy had at least eight on hand for skill training (one ball for every two players). We hadn't a clue where he got them from. They didn't belong to Riverside. They didn't belong to the school. Only Chippy knew, and he wasn't telling.

Chippy was heaped with praise. Pee Wee Flood gave him a few *Shoot* soccer magazines, told him to keep them. Nobby Clarke and Tootsie Devlin began cooing at him. Catho had gone as far as to invite him to his Da's restaurant for a free meal. There was a no chance of anything like that happening to Flintstone and me. We were ignored.

It got so bad we began to hate training.

Still we knew our chance of glory would come on match day. I still had my tracksuit from the street league and my fancy clobber. Whatever about training, I'd always look the part on match day, especially as Chippy wouldn't be around to capture the limelight. Match day would belong to the rest of us.

But we had a fight on our hands as Chippy began to take over more and more. Another few weeks and he'd be running the show. I'd end up as a linesman at best. More than likely I'd take over from Flintstone as team camel, carrying all the gear.

For a while we didn't know what to do. Then during an away match against Newtown, something happened that made us realise we'd have to do something. And fast.

There are plenty of hedges and ditches around the Newtown pitch and some big trees outside. The trees overlook the pitch so that if you could climb you wouldn't have to go in to watch the match; that's if you were daft enough to want to.

The match went as planned. Sean Mulligan put us a goal up after five minutes. Pee Wee Flood scored another a few minutes before half-time, scoring off a through ball played by Gemma Murphy out of defence. Pee Wee is good at that; scoring goals on the counter-attack, meaning he has pace and coolness. Coolness matters a lot. If you have it, you keep your nerve and slot goals home to perfection.

Most of the fun started at half-time.

This oul' lad came into the field, went over

to Newtown's manager. They began to row.

'What's the story?' Gypsy Walshe asked one of the Newtown players.

'It started a few weeks ago. It's been goin' on ever since. See yer man?'

'The oul' lad that just came in?'

'He was the manager, but ain't any more.'

'How come?'

'Committee threw him out. Gave the job to the fella he's rowin' with. Daft, isn't it?'

'Sure is. Two guys rowin' over one team.'

'It's typical adult male stupidity,' sniffed Gemma Murphy. The way she said it she sounded all grown-up. 'I mean, two grown men and they're arguing over a kids' football team. Kids wouldn't do the likes of that.'

That's where she was wrong. If Chippy kept on trying to take our team over we would have to defend our rights to the bitter end, Flintstone and me.

By now the two men were really shouting at one another. The referee and two other lads from Newtown had to separate them, tempers were that bad. In the end, they got the oul' lad outside. Told him not to come back in, that he was barred. Out. Out. Out!

But that didn't stop him. He climbed into one of the trees and watched from there. Not only did he watch. He caused plenty of aggro into the bargain, most of it directed at the new manager on the sideline.

Some people take football very seriously, just like the oul' lad in the tree. If we allowed Chippy to hang around our own team, much the same would probably happen, only Chippy wouldn't be daft enough to climb into a tree and make a show of himself.

For the record, we won the match 3-5. Pee Wee Flood again. Catho got the other.

We didn't bother saying goodbye to the oul' lad in the tree. See, he got stuck. We left that to someone with a ladder, a very long ladder.

Afterwards we went to see Mr Glynn and Harry. It took quite a while to persuade them to keep Chippy away from the team, but in the end we won the day. Chippy was told to keep away from then on.

Not that he cared. Just laughed it off.

5 Strip Trouble

There were no further letters. After the first two there was a sudden stop. At first I was slightly worried. Perhaps something had gone wrong for Victor and Henry, that's why there were no more letters. Then I changed my mind. I told myself that all of a sudden Victor and Henry had taken a liking to Birmingham, that they'd made new friends and couldn't care less if they never came back to Ireland.

There was one definite way I could have found out; I only had to write and ask what the story was. But I decided not to. I was afraid to, just in case I'd be flooded with another deluge of letters, all wanting to know if I'd got my sisters out of the house so as they (Victor and Henry) could come and live with us.

Lately, I'd become nice to my sisters. I became a real gentleman around the house, opening doors for them, asking if they'd like a cup of tea, had they seen any good pictures lately? I guess my conscience was at me, especially with Mad Victor putting the idea into my head to get rid of my sisters. I felt bad about that. At first, I didn't. But after having a good think I felt different. If I got rid of my sisters they'd end up on the streets, living in cardboard boxes, huddling in shop doorways at night, begging, the tears streaming down their faces. No, I couldn't be responsible for making my sisters homeless.

My conscience was at me all right, thanks to Victor and his spidery mis-spelt letters from Birmingham. Now if it were my Da I wouldn't have minded. I'd get rid of him any day. With him gone, there'd be room to sit down and watch the telly. It would be like having a new room in the house, maybe even as good as a new house.

The whole Victor and Henry scenario was a real dilemma.

The last letter from Birmingham had really touched me. Not only did Victor sign it; Henry did too. I could almost see tears in the writing.

The letter made me think hard about Victor and Henry, all the good times we had together. Especially Victor. How could I close the door in his face? Victor was important.

But he wasn't family.

Four weeks into the new season, we made a complaint to Mr Glynn. Four weeks! That's not bad, some teams never stop complaining. We only complain the odd time. Apart from Georgie, Ginger, Gypsy Walshe and Tootsie Devlin, we don't really have any cranks on the team. But not this time. Everyone was up in arms.

'What's up with the strip?' asked Pee Wee Flood of Mr Glynn.

'There's nothing wrong with it. It's perfect. Almost brand-new.'

'It's the same strip we wore with Dynamo Rouge.'

And it was. It still had Dynamo Rouge written on the crest.

'What are we supposed to do about that, Mr Glynn, the Dynamo Rouge? It's nothin' to do with Riverside Boys.'

'Take the crest off, that'll solve it.'

'But, Mr Glynn, it's an all-red strip, Riverside always wear claret and blue.'

'Minor point. Most of the other teams won't know the difference.'

'Wolfe Tone and Ardmore will. They're already sayin' we're a crowd of paupers, wearin' a second-hand strip.'

'So what? We can always say it's a change-strip.'

'Don't forget the Number Seven strip is missin'. Henry took it with him to Birmingham as a souvenir.'

I closed my eyes and pictured Henry in his Dynamo Rouge strip walking around Birmingham scrounging 50p pieces. Probably even doing his Irish dancing routine, something like the buskers in Grafton Street.

I was quickly brought back to earth. Mr Glynn was talking again:

'I'll buy a new Number Seven strip to replace Henry's. I'll pay for it out of my own pocket. Look, there aren't the funds to buy you a new strip. Any spare cash has to go towards the Youth team. A set of jerseys is a priority for them, as they haven't got any.'

We didn't have to hear any more. We were spot-on in deducing what Mr Glynn was on about. Catho, Gypsy Walshe and company would always be a hand-me-down team. They'd always be handed on a second-hand strip from an older team. Only for Terry O'Sullivan (Victor and Henry's step-da) donating the Dynamo Rouge strip, they'd probably have been landed with the strip my old team wore before the break-up.

That would have been a disaster for the present lot. They would have looked daft in our old strip. Only the likes of Nobby Roche and Sean Mulligan were big enough to be a proper fit. All the others would have been swallowed up by the sheer size of it. The only thing to be seen would be the strip, running around the field, tripping over itself. What a show! Georgie and Ginger would be on their bikes, gone back to Ardmore, rapid.

When Terry O'Sullivan donated the new strip to Dynamo Rouge he certainly did them a long-term favour.

Terry O'Sullivan: the Man from Jamaica.

What a guy!

6 Promotion!

One evening after training in the Park, Mr Glynn called me to one side. He wanted a word in private, meaning he didn't want the others to hear. I remember it well; it was the night after Chippy lit a bonfire near the street light where we train. How do I remember? Well, just like what happened on the Little Sugarloaf, most of the players got a good blackening from the charcoal of the bonfire. What with the black faces and the darkness it was hard to recognise who was who, that's except for the accents. Most of our lads have a funny way of talking. If you went blind overnight, you'd still know who you were talking to without being told.

We went over to one of the trees beside the path.

'Jimmy, I've a bit of a problem.'

'Like what, Mr Glynn?'

I wasn't really worried about Mr Glynn's problem. We all have problems. Harry

Hennessy has problems, Flintstone too. We've so many problems we couldn't care less any more. Another problem! So what? What's new?

'You're doing a great job, Jimmy. So good, you're capable of running the U-10s on your own. I'm very tied for time lately. And I'm thinking of having a light training session for the Youths on Saturday mornings, more to discuss pre-match tactics. That'd rule me out with the U-10s. Jimmy, would you take over the U-10s?'

'Sure, Mr Glynn! What about Flintstone?'

'Nothing to stop him from giving a dig-out. You'll need him anyway, as I'm keeping Harry with the Youths. Don't say a word to the players, not yet. I'll call a meeting at my house Friday night. We'll tell everyone then. It's for the better, Jimmy. This way, we can both give of our best.'

'Mr Glynn…how is Chippy getting on with the Youths?'

'Like a house on fire. He's coming right back to top form. The Dublin Schoolboys might even consider him for representative honours again, especially as Little Hitler has nothing to do with the Youth division. Maybe he's a bit too young this year. Next year, if his form holds, he should definitely be in with a chance...Now, remember the U-10s, my house, Friday night, seven-thirty sharp.'

We all turned up. That's except for Catho; he had cello lessons. His da always drives him there on a Friday night. Most times the cello can be seen sticking out the boot of the car, like part of a corpse wrapped in a body-bag. Luckily for Catho and his da the route they take isn't on Hot Pursuit's beat, because they'd end up in the barracks under suspicion of doing away with a body.

The reason the players, bar Catho, showed up for the meeting was because they thought they were going to a party. They sat two to an armchair, six on the sofa. Flintstone, Nobby Roche and I had an antique chair each. Mr Glynn sat in the middle of the room, where the coffee table usually is. Harry Hennessy had to stay in the hallway; there wasn't enough room.

But we didn't last long.

Mr Glynn left the room for a minute.

While he was gone, Mrs Glynn came in. She nearly died of shock when she saw us all sitting there.

Well, nearly all.

Gypsy Walshe had gone upstairs to mess with the bathroom taps. We could hear the water flowing ninety.

'Mr Glynn needs a plumber,' said Noel Cleary, our outside-left. 'My da's a good plumber.'

'Naw, it's only Gypsy messin'. It'll stop soon enough. He'll be back down in a sec.'

Tootsie Devlin had also vanished. He wandered into the kitchen, opened the fridge door and helped himself to a bowl of Mrs Glynn's prime trifle.

'What are you lot doing here?' asked Mrs Glynn.

'Waitin' to have a meetin', Mrs Glynn. A football meetin'.'

'Where's my husband?'

'He went outside to the garage for a few spare chairs.'

'Well, they can stay there!' fumed Mrs Glynn. 'Along with you lot! Get out of here! Don't come back!'

We took Mrs Glynn at her word, Gypsy and Tootsie included. We went out to the garage and held the meeting there. It was a bit crammed. But we managed. At least, there was an electric light, meaning we didn't have to talk to one another in the dark.

One plus: Harry Hennessy was able to stand just inside the door. The way he was standing made the meeting very important and official looking. It also gave the impression that Harry was in place to keep anyone who'd nothing to do with the team out. Mrs Glynn for instance.

When Mr Glynn told everyone that he and Harry Hennessy were giving up the U-10s and allowing me and Flintstone to take over, Georgie O'Connor and Ginger Mullin went ape.

'You can't do that, Mr Glynn!' moaned Georgie. 'We only joined because you were manager. If you leave, we'll go back to Ardmore. Jimmy ain't a proper manager. Half the team won't do what he tells them, not us anyway. There's no reason to leave, Mr Glynn. It's not that we're no good. Look, we've won all our matches so far. There's no point in leavin'.'

'I can't run both teams,' pleaded Mr Glynn. 'It's impossible. The fixtures and training clash too much. Jimmy's well able to do the job. He did really well in the street-league.'

'Not for us, Mr Glynn. We played for Ardmore in the street-league. And we won. If you don't stay, Mr Glynn, me and Ginger are leavin'.'

Georgie's words didn't do my pride any

good. But what worried me more was that Sean Mulligan might also ask for a transfer. Then we'd really start leaking goals and losing games. Maybe the two girls would also want to leave and join a girls team instead. If all that was to happen the team wouldn't be worth a monkey's curse.

Luckily there was no need to worry about Sean Mulligan, the two girls, or anyone else for that matter. They all said they'd stay no matter what. So my only worry was Georgie and Ginger.

7 Chippy has an Idea

Soon as the meeting was over I got working on a solution. I swallowed my pride and went to Chippy for help. Chippy being crafty, I reckoned he'd come up with a scam that'd keep Georgie and Ginger playing for Riverside, with me as manager.

I wasn't long giving him the lowdown.

'There's a way out,' smiled Chippy. 'Only last week I was talkin' to Brains O'Mahony.'

'How can Brains O'Mahony help? Brains O'Mahony knows nothin' about football.'

'He's lookin' for someone to do him a favour.'

'Like what?'

'Go and see him. Only when he asks for the favour, ask for one in return. Like you want him to get someone to let on they're a scout for Tottenham Hotspur.'

'Why a Tottenham scout?'

'Georgie and Ginger are mad Tottenham fans, aren't they? Tell them you're havin' them watched by a Spurs scout. That way they'll never leave, not unless Tottenham sign them, and that won't happen.'

'Think it'll work?'

'Of course. It's foolproof. You'd want to see Brains quick before he lines up someone else to do his favour. You'll catch him at the bus-stop beside Old Conna Avenue at eight in the morning. He gets the bus for Belfield there. Tell him I sent you.'

I felt a bit nervous about having a word with Brains, mainly because he's a lot older than any of us and has brains to burn. It's not easy talking to brainy people. But I was desperate to hold on to Georgie and Ginger.

Brains goes to college. University College Dublin is the name of it, though the place it's at is called Belfield. Brains has a university scarf and all. You'd think he lives at the North Pole the way he keeps it wrapped around his neck.

I got Brains the next morning standing at the bus-stop.

'What's up?' He asked.

'What d'ye mean, what's up?'

'There must be something. Only time I see

you lot is when there's something wrong.'

I was quick enough to tell Brains what was wrong. Quick enough in case the bus would come all of a sudden and I'd be left talking nonsense to myself at the bus-stop.'

'So you want me to line up someone who'll let on they're a football scout?'

'Yeah, a Tottenham scout.'

'And you'll do me a favour in return?'

'Sure. A favour for a favour.'

'There's this fella I know, Sean Gilroy from Sligo. He's doing a thesis on working-class social disorders.'

55

'What's that?'

'A thesis is a written document on a particular subject that a student has to write in order to get a degree.'

I didn't know what on earth he was on about but I choked back another 'what?'

'Where does the favour come in?' I asked, hoping I'd be able to understand the answer.

'Sean's short of material for his thesis, mainly because he hasn't much contact with working-class people. There's no such thing where he's from, not *urban* working-class. Reason being he's not from Sligo town, he's from out in the country.'

'Don't they work up there?'

'Yes, but they're farmers. Rural not urban. Now if you were to let him interview the likes of Mad Victor to research his thesis …'

'Mad Victor's out. He's away in Birmingham. No way Mad Victor can be interviewed.'

'What about Harry Hennessy?'

'What about him?'

'He's a real social problem, a social mess.'

'Harry's a changed man. Off the drink. The way he's goin' he wouldn't interest a flea.'

'There must be someone.'

And there was.

'Me da. He'd be a good subject. He's a real social mess.'

'Your da then. Think he'd sit down and be interviewed?'

'No. But we can trick him. It'll be easy.'

'Then I'll see Sean and tell him the story. I'm sure you can do a deal.'

'He'll have to show up now and again at matches. Just to make it look like he's a real football scout.'

'He'd have no objection to that.'

I waited another few minutes, until the bus came along. Thanks to Brains O'Mahony, your man from Sligo would be my saviour.

That night, at training, I told Georgie and Ginger all about the Tottenham scout that would be coming to watch them.

'Only thing, you'll have to stay with River-side,' I said.

'We'll stay.'

I had Georgie and Ginger in the bag. The problem, now, was to keep them there.

8 First Match Setback

A few days later I received another plea from the heart in the form of a letter from Mad Victor. He was really frantic, couldn't wait to come home, wanted to know if I'd finally got rid of my sisters, was it okay for him and Henry to come and live in my house.

With all the latest commotion surrounding the U-10s and being propelled into official league management, I'd forgotten all about Victor and Henry, but the worry was back full-time now. Some day soon they'd arrive back in Ireland, runaways from the terror of whatever it was that had them scared witless in Birmingham.

I weighed up the pros and the cons. On the pro side it would be good to see them back. We all missed Victor. Henry too. Football wise, Henry coming back would be a step in the right direction for the U-10s. His pace on the wing would help big time. Also, his accurate crossing, for Pee Wee Flood to work off and score a few extra goals.

On the con side there were the sisters.

I thought of writing Victor a long letter telling him I hadn't the heart to annoy my sisters so they'd leave home. That I couldn't do that, not to my family. I'd have to leave them be. But I couldn't get it right.

Instead I got a postcard of Bray Head and wrote a simple message: 'Can't get my sisters to leave. It's only getting me into trouble – I'll have to lay off. If you come home, make sure Henry brings his football boots. All the best, Jimmy.'

I added a PS: 'I might be able to put you up in the garden shed.'

I'd sent a written message to Victor and Henry. I'd also sent a hidden one. It wasn't by accident I'd selected the card with the photo of Bray Head on it. I was dropping a hint. That if everything failed they could live on Bray Head. Or they could become Eco Warriors and live in the trees. That would appeal to Victor and Henry; they just love being in trees.

After I sent the postcard I had a few words with Ma.

'Ma, can Victor and Henry live in the garden shed?'

'Why? They're in Birmingham, aren't they?'

'They're comin' back and have nowhere to live. The garden shed would be good enough until they got somewhere proper.'

'They couldn't live there, it's full of your father's stuff. We'd have to throw it all out to make room.'

That would suit me fine. Even better if he was thrown out too. He'd look well in a skip tied to a plank. He'd be the best bit of rubbish we ever got rid of.

'Ma, it'd only be for a while.'

'It's too cold in there. Anyway, they'd bring dogs about the place. They'd have them in the shed, the garden, everywhere.'

Ma was right. Victor and Henry are big dog lovers. They know more dogs than people.

I asked Ma one last time.

The answer: 'No! Definitely not!'

I had tried my best. I couldn't do any more.

By the following weekend, I was driven spare by Georgie and Ginger pestering me as to when the Tottenham (Spurs) scout would be coming to give them the once-over. They went on so much about the Spurs scout that the whole team knew about it, not to mention all their friends around Bray. What's more, it was having an effect on the rest of the players, that's except for Catho; he was too wrapped up in the world of music. The only lot he really wanted to play with was some posh orchestra that performed classical music.

On Sunday, we were at home to Rathnew. I couldn't give the pre-match pep talk without being nagged. At my first game as manager!

'Is yer man here?'

'Who?'

'The Spurs scout.'

'Not that I know. How'd I know what he looks like? He only sent word he'd be coming sometime soon. I wasn't supposed to tell you. I'm supposed to keep it a secret.'

Such a daft question. It was obvious there was no Spurs scout at the match. There were only the Rathnew lads, the ref and a few of Gypsy Walshe's pals who had nothing better to do.

Just before kick-off Pee Wee Flood started.

'I'm better than Georgie and Ginger. How come the scout's not comin' to look at me? I should be looked at!'

'Me too.' This time it was Baby Joe McCann.

'Baby Joe, you're only eight. You're too young. Spurs don't sign eight-year-olds.'

'If that's the case, they don't sign ten-year-olds either!'

Baby Joe was one smart eight-year-old. Too smart for my liking.

'Baby Joe,' I said, 'they won't be signing Georgie or Ginger. They'll only be looking. Maybe, when they turn thirteen, they'll bring 'em over to England to play in an under-age tournament. Build up the link. Then, when they're old enough, they'll sign them. That's the way they do it with under-age players.'

'Some big deal,' sniggered Tootsie Devlin. 'They'd be savin' more if they signed them before fourteen. They'd be able to bring 'em over for half fare.'

'Real smart, Tootsie,' seethed Nobby Roche. 'You'll be goin' nowhere, 'cause ye're not good enough.'

'Neither will you or Georgie or Ginger. It's all a cod. A ready-up.'

I was quick to react; I had to be.

'No, it's not! It's goin' to happen.'

'When?'

'Next week, the week after. The Tottenham scout is definitely coming. He's been in touch. He's lots of other lads to look at. We just have to wait our turn, that's all.'

I had trouble getting the players out on to the pitch. They were hyper with all the talk about the Spurs scout. Flintstone and I had to calm them. Then the referee was on the centre-spot with Rathnew Celtic, waiting for Riverside to line up for the kick-off. It hurt my pride like hell being late on the pitch.

We were all upset going into the match. All upset rowing over the Spurs scout, and who was good enough, and who wasn't good enough, to play for Spurs at White Hart Lane.

After ten minutes we settled. Pee Wee Flood scored a gem of a goal, the type any Tottenham centre forward would be proud of.

But Rathnew had already scored two. Both in the first five minutes.

Only for Sean Mulligan at centre-half the scoreline could have been worse. He steadied the ship. Got us back on course. Him, Catho and Gemma Murphy.

We ended up getting beaten 2-3. I'd lost my first match in charge.

And that wasn't the only upset.

Late in the second half Ginger Mullin got into a row with one of the Rathnew players. They collided going for a fifty-fifty ball. They began to pull at each other. Then the slagging started.

'Your brother thumped my brother five years ago!' roared the Rathnew lad. He was

fed up with Ginger, really fed up.

'He did not!'

'He did!'

'How d'ye know it was me brother?'

'He had red hair, just like you. Red hair and a big mouth!'

Only the referee got between them there would have been serious trouble.

The slagging continued.

'All ye're good for is lockin' up refs in the boots of cars!'

'That wasn't us. That was St Earnan's! We're not Earnan's.'

'Ye're all one and the same. Rathnew for soccer; Earnan's for Gaelic.'

'What are ye on about? That was over thirty years ago. Anyway, it probably wasn't Earnan's that locked the ref in the boot. It was some other club. Ye're all muddled, ye nutter!'

History isn't easily forgotten. Not by Rathnew.

Certainly not by Riverside boys.

Soon as the game ended, I headed straight for Brains O'Mahony's house.

I wanted the Tottenham scout in Bray for

our next home game, against Kilcoole.

I had thought of getting him sooner. But we were away to a team whose pitch was up a warren of country lanes. Your man from Sligo wouldn't have a clue of the area, even if I drew a map. He'd probably get lost, regardless of being brainy and going to college.

Anyway I worked it all out with Brains O'Mahony. The Sligo Wonder would definitely be in Bray in two weeks time.

I could hardly wait.

Neither could Georgie and Ginger and – unfortunately – the whole team.

I'd started an epidemic. An 'I-want-to-play-for-Tottenham-Hotspur' epidemic.

I had a feeling a big crowd would show up. More to see the Spurs scout than to watch Riverside play.

We'd have made a fortune if we could have charged in.

But who'd pay money to watch Riverside?

Not the nippers from Palermo, or anywhere else for that matter.

In the end, everyone got to see the Tottenham scout for free.

9 Spurs Night

The Tottenham scout was on most of the players' minds all week. I tried to calm the situation but it was only a waste of time. They kept on questioning me about Tottenham Hotspur's history; how they started out, who were their most famous players, how they'd done over the years. In fact, almost everything to do with the club's history.

I was worried they wouldn't be able to concentrate on the upcoming weekend match, away to the team that hung out in the middle of a maze of country laneways. I don't want to mention the team by name, they might take offence. But they were real country lads, straight from the land that time forgot.

I hadn't a clue what to say, so I went to see Chippy. He'd probably know how to sort the mess out.

'Thursday evening call "Spurs Night". Tell the players you'll answer all their question then. That way, they won't pester you any more and you can concentrate on Sunday's match in peace.'

'Sounds like a good idea. Only I know nothing about Spurs.'

'You don't have to. Go and see Oul' Fred, he's the biggest Spurs fan alive. He's got all their match programmes goin' back years. His mind's full of Tottenham Hotspur. Ask him to take charge of the Spurs Night. He'll probably let you use his house. Youse can sit on the programmes if there's not enough chairs.'

Knowing Oul' Fred well, I though Chippy's idea was brilliant. We'd got to know Oul' Fred over the years when sheltering from the rain in his doorway after being up the town. He lives on his own with two cats, a half-blind Labrador and his Tottenham Hotspur mementos. His doorway is one of the biggest in Bray. There's enough room for four lads to sit down and play a game of poker. In fact, there's enough room for Victor and Henry to live there, that's if Oul' Fred would give them permission, which he wouldn't.

The Spurs Night went a treat. Oul' Fred was only too delighted to have us all over to his

house. He said he once knew Jimmy Greaves.

'Who's Jimmy Greaves?'

'He played for Spurs and England. He lost out in the 1966 World Cup Final to Geoff Hurst. Hurst scored a hat trick. Jimmy would have scored six. He's a Cockney.'

'Wha's a Cockney?'

'A fella that's lived all his life in London, an' speaks with a Cockney accent. It's no use just livin' in London; you've to have the accent.'

I'd been told sometimes Oul' Fred puts on a Cockney accent. It all depends how Tottenham are doing in the Cup. See, Tottenham's not a

League team any more; they're a Cup team.

Glory, Glory, Halleluia!
Glory, Glory, Halleluia!
Glory, Glory, Halleluia!
And the Spurs go marching on!

He also told us about Joe Kinnear who played for Spurs. 'There's a great Spurs book, *The Glory Game* – Joe gets a mention in it. He bought his granny back in Dublin a telly, so as she could watch him on 'Match of the Day'. I think he bought her an armchair as well ....'

We got Tottenham Hotspur for two hours. Those of us who had the brain to take it all in ended up experts on the club. Oul' Fred hardly halted to take in breath. He must have been the greatest Spurs fan going.

I found out later that once when Spurs came to Dublin to play a friendly, Fred went along in his Tottenham gear and got to sit on the bench next to the subs, hoping that they'd think he was some new player the manager wanted to try out. If he'd been sitting there forty years earlier there's a chance he'd have got away with it, but age shows. The stewards were called and he was put back in with the crowd where he belonged. But he didn't do badly; he got to sit in the stand right next to some big-wheel Tottenham director.

Oul' Fred always does something special when Tottenham are in town. Chippy says that's why they don't come to Ireland very often. They're afraid Oul' Fred will show up.

I was certainly glad we all went to Fred's for Spurs Night. The whole experience calmed my players a treat. Now that they knew all about Tottenham the nagging died down. I'd got them off my back for a while. Anyway, they'd get a taste of the real thing in a week's time in the form of your man from Sligo. I could only hope he'd look the part.

And why wouldn't he?

All football scouts look the part.

Your man from Sligo wouldn't prove any different.

10 New Blood

On Sunday, we played the team from the country laneways. We travelled by CIE and the bus left us at the bottom of one of the lanes, meaning we had to walk almost a mile. There were signs on the hedges pointing out the way to the pitch. Most of the other team passed us by, two and three to a bike.

The pitch wasn't much. The opposition likewise. We won 0-4. But it proved a real landmark for me: my first win as a manager in an official league. I didn't mind the walk back down the laneways after the match, or the half-hour wait for the bus home. I was over the moon. I felt as if I'd just conquered the world.

I was so elated that next day I toured most of the housing estates in Bray on the lookout for some fresh talent for the Kilcoole match.

It probably would have been easier to poach some players off another team, but having got Georgie and Ginger from Ardmore, and beaten clubs like Wolfe Tone and St

Fergals to Sean Mulligan's signature on a registration form. I preferred to look around and pick up a few players the other clubs didn't know about, new lads that had only moved to Bray.

I cycled around all the estates, looking for patches of grass suitable for playing football. I wasn't into lads playing on the road. I had to see them play on grass, because that's where real football matches are played; on grass, not a hard road surface.

I know all about the difference between grass and roads. Some lads are great at playing football on the road, but put them on grass and they freeze, can't play at all. It's the same in other ways. A few lads are stars playing in their clothes, but put a football kit on them and they fall apart. Some can only play in their shoes – give them football boots and they can't kick a ball out of their way. I wanted lads playing on grass and wearing proper football gear.

I spent three days after school going around.

First day, there was no one out playing football. I had to make a few enquires at school as to when was the best time to catch them.

Second day, I caught some of them.

Third day, I got the remainder.

Most of them already played for clubs, or were the wrong age. The remainder were probably 'sunshine footballers', lads who only played when the sun shone. A sniff of rain or cold weather and they wouldn't show up. They'd only be a waste of time.

By teatime Wednesday I'd given up. Then, out of the blue, this fellow named Tomser from Wolfe Tone knocked on my door.

'Hear you're lookin' for a few good players.'

'Yeah, know one?'

'There's this fella new to Bray, used to live in Stillorgan. He plays anywhere across the back four or central-midfield.'

'How d'ye know?'

'I've seen him play... I've seen your team play. I know what you're after. Thought I'd do you a good turn, tell you about him.'

'Why the good turn? I don't know you.'

'I played for Riverside once. Just like to do a good turn, that's all... I hear a Spurs scout is watchin' your team. Couldn't get me a few autographs of Spurs players, could you?'

I could. All I'd have to do is see Chippy. He loves signing autographs. He'd do the whole Spurs squad, properly spelt and presented.

'What's this lad's name?'

'Dave Doherty. He lives near Wolfe Tone. Hangs around with some of the Toners. I've seen him kicking about with them.'

'How come, if he's so good, he's not playin' for them?'

'The manager doesn't know about him – he still goes to school in Stillorgan. He's never been in the field when the manager's there. The Wolfe Tones don't want the manager to see him, in case he gets one of their places.'

Wolfe Toners are like that. They don't like outsiders to take over from them.

'What's his address?'

Soon as Tomser gave me the address I was on Harry Hennessy's bike like a light, off up the Vevay, knocking on the young lad's door. An hour later I had him on a patch of grass under a street light for a kickabout with me, Chippy and Flintstone. He looked a good one. I signed him on the spot and put him on the panel for Sunday's game against Kilcoole.

Afterwards I gave him a crossbar home.

'I gotta friend,' he said.

'Where does he live?'

'Stillorgan. Only he comes and stays with me every weekend. We go to school together. Mind if I bring him along on Sunday?'

'Not half, what's his name?'

'Robbie Ryan. Plays midfield or up front.'

'Is he any good?'

'Yeah, about the same as me.'

Just when I thought we would be struggling against the top teams in the league. I had come across two great new players.

That's what I like about football most; it's full of surprises. We'd surprise Wolfe Tone – with one of their own.

11 The Scout Shows Up

The Tottenham scout showed up for the match against Kilcoole in the Park.

He arrived on a red Honda scooter. Just like Brains, he had a UCD scarf hoisted around his neck. Unlike Brains, he also had a pair of goggles and a motor-bike helmet. There was a right crowd in the Park to witness his arrival. Some even had scraps of paper to get his autograph.

Dave Doherty, the new player I'd just signed was also there. He had his football gear at the ready. I'd start him at left-full, see how he got on there. Maybe after a few matches, move him to play beside Sean Mulligan at centre-half and switch Baby Joe McCann to the left-full slot. Baby Joe is a masterful player, but at eight he'd progress better playing as a full-back. Dave Doherty had his mate Robbie from Stillorgan with him. Just as the Tottenham scout arrived he was having a kickabout with some of the lads. He looked useful, had bags of skill, and a humdinger of a shot. I'd get him signed rapid and have him out on the pitch as a Riverside player the following week.

The Tottenham scout parked the Honda beside one of the trees. He took his helmet and goggles off and had a good look around.

He spotted me straightaway.

'I'm Sean Gilroy,' he said. 'Pleased to meet you.'

'Pleased to meet you,' I answered, offering my hand. He didn't look much like a football scout, not with the Honda and accessories. Already he was setting off the wrong vibes withPee Wee Flood. Gypsy Walshe, too, was getting a right laugh out of it. The Spurs scout arriving on a miserable Honda scooter! It wasn't even as if it was new, it was an old banger. As for the monster-sized scarf, it didn't look remotely like Tottenham gear.

Georgie and Ginger came over like a light.

'That's him, isn't it, the Spurs scout?'

'Yeah, but you're not supposed to know,' I half whispered. 'Scouts don't like players knowin' in advance they're bein' watched.'

'Why did you tell us then? Introduce us.'

I had no choice, especially as they were standing right next to the Spurs scout, smiling starry-eyed into his face.

Soon as I made the introduction, they handed him their names and addresses on a scrap of paper.

'Just in case,' Ginger said. 'We'd hate to think we'd made it and couldn't be found. That'd break our hearts. Wouldn't it Georgie?'

'Sure, Mister. Kilcoole's crap. Our players are mostly crap. We're the only good things around here. Just lettin' you know, so you won't be wastin' your time.'

'I'm certain you're up to scratch. We'll have you off to the Showgrounds in no time.'

'The showgrounds?'

'He means White Hart Lane.'

Brains had told me your man was a Sligo Rover fan. Him and his Showgrounds! I didn't think he'd be that much of a Sligo Rovers fanatic. Georgie and Ginger wouldn't think much of being bundled off to the Showgrounds in Sligo. If that was the case, they'd be better off with Bray Wanderers. At least, they'd save on time and train fares.

After that, I had to take your man to one side and remind him he was a Spurs scout.

'D'ye know much about Tottenham?'

'Sure.'

'Where they play and all that.'

'Of course. Dave McKay, Danny Blanchflower, Alan Gilzean, Glenn Hoddle and Ossie Ardilles. Sure, I know all about Spurs.'

'Lay off the Sligo bit then. All they want to know about is Spurs. Those two would give their right arms to play for Spurs.'

'Aren't they a bit too young?'

'They think Spurs might sign them when

they're older. If not, they're gonna leave me and join another schoolboy team. That's what this is all about. I wanna keep them here. You just show up now and again, keep the thing goin'. Tell them you have to make progress reports back to Tottenham, that you'll sign them in a few years time.'

'A few years! If you think I'm comin' back here for a few years, you're mistaken.'

'Just show up once or twice. Disappear after that. Tell them you've to go missin' for a year, but you'll be back. Once you do the business a few times everything will be all right.'

'When do I get to interview your da for my thesis?'

What with everything on my mind I'd forgotten what a thesis was. I had to ask again.

'No big deal. Just a paper I've to do on working-class people, ambition and the likes.'

'My da doesn't have any ambition.'

'That's what makes him perfect. He's just what I want. Someone stuck in a rut, not wanting to make anything of himself.'

'That's my da.'

'Like I said, when can I interview him?'

'Soon as I set it up. Gotta phone number?'

'Sure.'

Luckily I had a biro with me to fill in the referee's card. I wrote his phone number down. Then I gave him my number, mainly because we'd got a phone lately and I wanted to show off a bit.

Our new phone was the talk of the neighbourhood. We could have got a mobile, which would have been niftier. But Da wanted the real thing. A mobile is handed to you; when it's a real phone a van is sent around to install it. That way the neighbours get to know and Da wanted the neighbours to know. Instead of one van we got two, and a lorry. Da didn't have to pay a penny. He worked some scam and got the job done for nothing.

One point I made clear to Sean Gilroy:

'When you ring, ask for Jimmy Quinn *Junior*. Da's got the same name as me. There could be a mix-up. Make sure you add the junior bit.'

And there was a mix-up once. When I was seven a poem of mine was published in the local paper. It was all about a mouse looking out through a mouse-hole. Most of the neighbours thought the poem was written by Da. For a while, they thought he'd gone a bit mental. He felt so embarrassed he refused to leave the house for a week. He told me to send no more poems to the papers, especially poems signed by Jimmy Quinn.

Me, I couldn't wait to write another, that's if I got the right inspiration. But matters didn't work out. Da went to the newspaper office and told the staff not to print any more poems by me, that it wasn't in keeping with his public image. That was choice! See, Da doesn't have a public image, not the right one anyway. What's more, he's not a patch on me when it comes to writing. The only thing he's capable of writing is his signature in the dole office. Even that's not great. It's spidery, like what would look cool pinned to Mrs O'Leary's door at Halloween.

Once the match started I had the Tottenham scout stand nice and prominent so as all the players could see him. I gave him my biro and a sheet of paper, told him to take a few notes on how the players were performing, that it would make him look the real thing.

Talking about the real thing. I told him to stuff the UCD scarf into his pocket and leave the helmet lying on the ground, that he wouldn't look so daft. Only problem was, he was wearing an anorak with the hood up. It made him look like an Eskimo on holidays. But I didn't bother saying that to him, as I didn't want to hurt his feelings.

What am I saying? I didn't want him to walk off in a huff.

The match went a treat. Everybody played well, including Kilcoole. Our latest addition, Dave Doherty, had played well without being flash. I could hardly wait to put his friend, Robbie Ryan, out on the pitch the following week. Having them made the squad very strong. I could see us troubling the top teams in the league, possibly beating them.

We won the match 2-1. Only problem for Georgie and Ginger was they thought the lad who side-footed the Kilcoole goal was the best player. It troubled them greatly.

'The Spurs scout won't bother with us, he'll go for your man.'

'No, he won't,' I assured them. 'Influence counts. I've plenty of that. Stay with me and you can't go wrong.' I could hardly believe my ears. I'd begun to act like Chippy; a pure chancer! 'Stay put with Riverside and I'll see to it you get trials with Spurs soon enough.'

I spoke with heart. I really convinced them.

Your man from Sligo also tackled me. He began rattling away about the thesis and getting an interview with Da. Luckily I got rid of him without the others finding out. He drove off on his Honda into the gathering darkness. I wasn't half glad to see the back of him.

Pity I wasn't able to get away from Georgie and Ginger as easily.

They were a right pain in the neck.

12 The Interview

Robbie Ryan made his debut for Riverside U-10s the weekend before Halloween. I played him up front alongside Pee Wee Flood. He played a blinder. What's more, we won again.

Dave Doherty was a treat too. He played even better than in his debut game. I'd have the choice of playing him in several positions, centre-half or central midfield possibly being his best. That went for Robbie too.

At last, there was balance to the team. The panel was strong, plenty of cover for each position, except goalkeeper. Nobby Roche was good, improving by the game, but there was no backup if he were injured. At that, I wasn't entirely without options, Pee Wee Flood was a class goalkeeper, only he'd be wasted in goal, especially as he was a top class goal poacher. Still, if need be, he'd fill the void if required. There was backup for Pee Wee at centre-forward. Like I've said, the panel was strong. Options were no problem.

On Halloween night someone knocked on the hall door.

'Don't answer it,' ordered Da. 'It's only the kids lookin' for apples and nuts.'

He had his feet up, right next to the fire, reading *The Racing Post*.

I thought I'd answer the door anyway. See I knew your man from Sligo was due. He told me he'd call at Halloween. He said he liked being out and about on Halloween night. I guess, being from Sligo, superstition was in his blood. Years ago my Granda told me everyone from the West of Ireland is superstitious, that Sligo is a hotbed for superstition. It's something to do with the rain, the mist, the damp, and the fairies.

I was in Sligo once. We went on a school tour to the Lake Isle of Innisfree. The wind off the lake was freezing cold. Why your man Yeats wanted to go and live there beats me. There's hardly enough room to swing a cat, let alone build a cabin. It's that lonely, you'd definitely crack up. Not even Flintstone would be able to put up with the loneliness and he can put up with almost anything. He can live on fresh air, can Flintstone. There's plenty of that on the Lake Isle of Innisfree.

The scenery was good though.

Only problem, you can't eat scenery.

Anyway, your man from Sligo (the Tottenham scout) came knocking on the hall door. It was 7.30 in the evening. Da was settled in for the night. Ma was doing the washing-up. My two sisters were getting ready to go on the prowl for steady boyfriends.

Me, I was all excited. I had been peeping out through the curtains to see if your man from Sligo was coming.

When the knock came, I was out to the door in a flash.

'Come on in,' I said. 'Come into the sitting room. I'll bring Da in there in a minute.'

'Does he know I'm coming?'

'Sure, I told him a few days ago. I said there was a reporter from *The Racing Post* wanting to interview him. He can't wait, says it's a real privilege. He's even dressed up. Don't forget, make sure he thinks you're from *The Racing Post*. If not, he won't co-operate. He'll sulk and won't want to know. See you in a sec.'

I went and got Da up off the armchair, the only one in the kitchen. Nobody else was allowed to sit there, not even the cat.

'Da, the man from *The Racing Post* is here. He's in the sitting room, all ready and waitin' to go.'

'Has he got a pen and paper?'

'Course he has, Da. He's a reporter you know. Pen and paper are the tools of his trade. Reporters don't go anywhere without pen and paper.'

'Let's go then.'

'What d'ye mean?'

'You come with me. Keep me company.'

'You'll have your man, he'll be there. It won't be like you'll be talkin' to yourself. Your man will be all ears.'

Da insisted I went with him. He's like that, my da. Once there are strangers about he feels insecure. It's a real problem for him. He finds it hard to cope with strangers. Just as we were leaving the kitchen for the sitting room my two sisters came downstairs.

'Da, we're goin' out. There's a party on, we'll be back late.'

Before they left, I introduced them to your man from Sligo, just in case he might take a fancy to one of them and fall in love.

'I like the way they're done up for Halloween,' commented your man from Sligo.

'They're like that all the time.'

My sisters had left the house before that exchange. If they'd heard my remark, I'd have been the one to leave the house – through the door as quick as a greyhound out of a trap.

I introduced Da.

There was a print of a racehorse over the mantelpiece. It was Da's favourite. The only racehorse he'd won real money on.

'That's Arkle, remember him?'

'Sure.' He didn't sound at all sure. I hoped Da would reflect it was a stupid question to put to a racing correspondent.

Although he was long before my time, even *I'd* heard of Arkle. In fact, I'm still hearing about him. He's the one piece of history I know all about, though he'll never show up on any exam paper. When it comes to Arkle, I'm one of the world's leading experts, thanks to Da.

The three of us sat down at the low table before the fireplace, meaning I got in on the interview.

At first it was awkward for the Sligo lad to take notes. But Da quickly solved the problem. He piled three telephone directories on top of the table. That meant the Sligo lad didn't have to stoop much when taking notes, once Arkle was out of the way.

The interview went along as follows:

'Do you mind living in a council house?'

'Why should I? It's like any other house.'

'What time do you get up in the morning?'

Silence.

'Do you miss having a regular job?'

More silence.

'Do you aspire to improve your lot in life?'

'Wha' d'ye mean?'

'Say, working full-time, increasing your income, having a better style of living, that kind of betterment.'

'Wha' d'ye mean? I'm fine. No stress, no worries. Why rock the boat? Only mess things up. I'm happy enough the way things are.'

'At what age did you leave school?'

'Wha's that to do with *The Racing Post* and horse-racing?'

'Your family background, was it always as it is now?'

Da had begun to smell a rat. Not only that; he was looking it straight in the face.

'Hey, wha's up with you? Why all the nosy questions? Wha's that scarf doin' wrapped around your neck? It's a university scarf, isn't it? You're a student, out on a project. I suppose they're teaching you how to do interviews. You don't want to ask me about horse-racing at all. You're a rich geezer trying to take the mickey out of me…Jimmy, wha's this all about? Jimmy, you set this whole thing up?'

'I didn't, Da. I'm only doin' the man a favour. He's hard up. He hasn't even got a car. Only a Honda scooter. A ten-year-old one at that. Lay off, Da!'

'Jimmy, wha's in this for you? Wha' are you gettin' out of it?'

All I was going to get was the hope that Georgie and Ginger would stay put with Riverside. But how could I get that through to Da. See, he isn't a football man. He wouldn't understand. So, I decided to save my breath. I didn't answer back. Just tried to make myself as dopey-looking as I could. Which wasn't hard.

Instead Da got stuck into your man from Sligo. He was backing him into a corner.

'I know all about interviews, that sort of caper. Don't "intimidate" the "interviewee". Don't look directly into his face, relax him. Don't be over informal. I went through it all. Only it wasn't at college. It was down at FÁS They even had us talking into bananas, letting

93

on they were telephones. That's the university education I got. Bloody humiliation! An' you goin' on about self-improvement! That's not on here. Jimmy, show him the door!'

I wasn't long getting your man from Sligo out of the house. He was fairly shook up; he didn't want to come back.

'Da's usually quiet. Come back next week. It'll be different.'

But I couldn't change your man's mind.

'What'll we do about Georgie and Ginger?' I asked.

'Georgie and Ginger?'

'The two lads that think you're watchin' them for Tottenham.'

'Get someone else to watch them.'

I managed to talk the Tottenham scout (he wasn't your man from Sligo any more) out of it. I told him I knew all about Da. I said I'd fill in the interview for him. That we could meet a week later in Abrakebabra and I'd do the business, that he'd have no bother completing his thesis. I swore I'd give him the best low-down on dossers that anyone could ever get. I told him I'd put him on the map, no bother.

What with me being a writer I'd have no problem spinning a yarn – I knew I could add in a few extra juicy bits. I didn't tell the Tottenham scout that, just said I'd make it well worth his while.

He was impressed. He agreed to meet me one week later in Abrakebabra.

What's more, he said he'd come and watch Georgie and Ginger at least twice during the season, maybe tell them a few stories about White Hart Lane.

In the short term, the Tottenham scout would get enough material for his thesis.

Long term, I'd get to keep Georgie and Ginger.

The arrangement worked to a tee.

Both of us went home happy.

13 Junior Cert

Two weeks later, we'd a crunch match away to Ardmore. It proved to be one of the most important games of the season, especially as I was afraid Georgie and Ginger might still leave Riverside and go back to Ardmore. That's if they started to lose faith in the Tottenham scout.

Going into the match we had a setback. Catho wasn't available. He was off somewhere playing the cello at a posh concert. We couldn't understand how he'd turn down a crunch match to go off and play the cello in front of a lot of stuffy oul' wans.

As we walked to the Ardmore pitch I noticed Nobby Roche was nervous as hell.

'Nobby, it's only a match, take it easy.'

Gypsy Walshe had a different suggestion: 'Like a fag? It'll help settle your nerves.'

'He doesn't want a fag,' I snapped. 'If Mr Glynn heard you, he'd tell you to keep away from the team. He doesn't want any of this lot smokin'. What's more, they don't.'

And none of them did smoke, that's apart from Gypsy Walshe and Tootsie Devlin. Their families were chronic smokers; so much smoke came out of their windows that people often called the fire brigade.

Instead of a cigarette, I gave Nobby some of my Wrigley's chewing gum. It started a trend. After that, he always chewed gum during our matches. Sometimes he'd stick it to the goal-post to keep track of the score, especially when the lads were in top scoring form.

When we got to the pitch we soon realised why Nobby was so nervous.

Some of the Ardmore gang had spent the past weeks slagging him. It didn't take long for it to start at the pitch.

'Weighs a ton. Can't move, can he?'

'Course he can,' retorted Tootsie Devlin. 'He's a deadly goalkeeper. Nothin' gets by him. Bet you 20p you won't score. He'll stop everythin'.'

'20p?'

'Yeah.'

'You're on.'

So were five others. Tootsie Devlin was set to lose £1.20 if we let in a goal.

'Ye're goin' to lose,' whispered one of the lads to Tootsie.

'No, I'm not. I haven't got one pound twenty. I've only 5p. Lose and I'll take off just before the match ends. Win, an' I'll hang on, meanin' I'll be one pound twenty richer.'

Tootsie had everything worked out to a tee. He's as sharp as Chippy. It runs in his family. They're all tricksters, amongst the smartest in Bray.

As it was, Nobby didn't have to make many saves. We ran Ardmore ragged. They didn't know what hit them, more so because of the two new players, Dave Doherty and Robbie Ryan.

Robbie was sensational. Ardmore just couldn't handle him. They'd have nightmares over him for a week. The final rub was Nobby in goal. He brought off three top-notch saves and earned himself a reputation as well as making Tootsie Devlin £1.20 richer. See, we won 0-2.

The Ardmore game was important. It meant

we were on a winning run, confidence was high. All of a sudden, we knew we had a near-perfect team. Georgie and Ginger wouldn't be leaving in a hurry. The Tottenham scout was redundant; it probably wouldn't matter if he were to never show up again. From now on, I'd have their respect as a manager.

I was rapidly becoming the Alex Ferguson of schoolboy football.

While I'd turned things around for the U-10s, life wasn't as rosy for the Youth team. They found it hard to put a winning run together, dropping points on a regular basis.

Mr Glynn wasn't as lucky as I had been, he was finding it hard to come across the few star players who would have made all the difference and put the team in a winning groove. At Youth level it's hard to pick up class players once the season has begun because they're already spoken for, sounded out and signed in advance. But Mr Glynn would hang in and do his best with what he had. He'd keep his cool and work on organising the team as a unit, build on team spirit. He is one of the best schoolboy mangers in the game. Given time he'd improve the team's form. They'd never be a trophy-winning team, but they'd gain respect and become a match for the best.

Though he never said it, I think Mr Glynn was content to keep the team on a reasonably even keel, as long as Chippy remained with Riverside. He worked in the hope that he'd get Chippy back into the reckoning for underage representative honours. When he achieved that, he would be happy enough.

And Chippy was on his way back. His form was top class.

Way back in September we'd got our Junior Cert results. We'd got the day off school and had to go in that morning to collect the results.

Flintstone didn't bother going in. I collected for him. We were all given a slip of paper with the results typed out.

I didn't do too badly. Well, I passed.

Growler Hughes passed.

Chippy too.

We all passed. All except Flintstone.

We met Flintstone outside the school gate,

handed him his envelope.

He opened it, but he already feared the worst.

'Well, how did you do?'

He didn't answer. We could see tears in his eyes. Then he had a good cry.

Chippy took the results slip from Flintstone, and said, 'Mind if I tear this up?'

'No.'

Chippy tore the result slip into tiny pieces and trampled them on the ground. 'Forget about it. Just go home and say you didn't do too well. It isn't the end of the world.'

So saying, Chippy tore up his result slip and let it scatter on the wind.

He made us all do the same.

'That's it,' he said. 'Torn up, all gone. Life moves on. Let's get outa here. Maybe get the next Dart into Dublin an' have a good time.'

'Why Dublin?'

'Why not? It's a change, different, just what Flintstone needs right now. Who's comin'?'

We all were – the Riverside gang.

We trooped off to the railway station, took turns to take Flintstone's mind off being branded a failure.

Chippy did best.

We all admired him for that.

Regardless of what happened in the past, he was back in favour again.

A week later the Principal asked Flintstone to his office.

'It is best that your education takes a different direction.'

'Wha' d'ye mean, Sir?'

'You'd be best served leaving here and taking up an alternative education.'

'Like wha'?'

'Unfortunately your results don't warrant your staying on here, but there's a VEC course that would suit you. It's called Youth Reach. Consider it. Talk it over with your parents before making a decision. I'd recommend it. You can let me know in a few days time.'

Flintstone decided he'd go on the VEC course. The school was in the Vevay, at Sunbeam House. It was a two-year course.

'Think you'll stick it, Flintstone?'

'Yeah. They give us a few quid. For a few quid I'd stick anythin'.'

Flintstone sounded as if he liked the new school. Two weeks later he'd forgotten all about the disappointment of the Junior Cert.

When he settled in I got around to asking him more questions.

'Still goin' well at the new school?'

'We get a free lunch. Anywhere that gives a free lunch has to be good. And we have to call the teachers by their first name. One is Des – he teaches woodwork and brings us off playin' football and adventure sports. We were in Clara-Lara last week. There's no such thing as bein' given out to, nothin'. Most of the lads are daft, but they all get on well with the teachers.'

'What is it, a holiday camp?'

'No, we do all kinds of things. We do cookin', photography, video, drama and work experience, even buildin' skills. It's not like ordinary school.'

'Sounds great. Victor would have liked the video. You must be havin' a ball.'

'Not really. There's maths and English too.'

That was hardship. Flintstone's a dead loss at maths; English as well, apart from being able to speak the stuff.

Anyway, it was good to see him getting back to himself.

What was even better, he was a lot happier going off in the morning to the new school. You could see it in the way he walked. He fairly bounced along the road.

Pity Victor was gone off to Birmingham, the new school would have suited him too. What with his video skills and all. It was a waste, Victor being in Birmingham. If he'd stayed in Bray, Youth Reach could have turned him into a world-famous film director. Victor would be a great man for making cowboy films – once he had the cowboys to act the part.

He knows all about cowboys.

Once Chippy and me had a row over which cowboy got shot in the back playing poker.

'It was Wild Bill Hickock,' said Chippy.

'Naw, Wyatt Earp.'

'Wild Bill Hickock. He had a thing about sittin' with his back to the saloon door. In the end that's just what he did, an' he got shot.'

'You don't say?'

'I do. It was Wild Bill Hickock!'

Around about then Mad Victor came along.

'Victor, which cowboy got shot in the back playin' poker?'

'Wild Bill Hickock. Ever heard of a Dead-man's Hand? Well, that's what Wild Bill had in his hand. Wild Bill Hickock's yer man.'

Victor!

We still missed Victor.

I hadn't heard from him lately. I wondered was he settling down?

I wouldn't have to wonder much longer, I was about to find out.

14 Return of the Natives

They say life is full of surprises. Well, I had two in the next week – two bombshells.

The first surprise was on a Sunday afternoon, soon as I got home after being off with the U-10s playing Ashford. The surprise would have happened earlier in the day, only Da doesn't get up until 12.30 on a Sunday morning, meaning he doesn't get to read the *Sunday World* until 1 o'clock.

It took Da ten minutes to come across the surprise. It was on page twelve of the *Sunday World*, almost a whole page of a surprise. In my case I didn't have to turn the pages to find it. It was spread on the kitchen table, just waiting for me to come home.

'Come here, you!' Da thundered, soon as I walked in. His thunder was so loud, I was full certain lightning would follow.

He brought me into the kitchen, pointed out page twelve of the *Sunday World*. 'You! You've disgraced me!'

I stood rooted to the spot. Page twelve was bad, real bad. There was a huge headline and a picture of our house. And Da was raving and ranting about how I'd made a show of the family by bringing the so-called Tottenham scout around to the house.

The headline seemed to get larger by the second. The photo too looked as if it would become real any minute and Da would come charging out, baying for my blood.

The headline read: IRELAND'S BIGGEST DOSSER!

The caption below the picture: DOSSER'S 'HOME SWEET HOME'!

Da called Ma and my sisters into the kitchen. He made us all sit down and told Ma to read the article aloud.

There were plenty of juicy bits in it, more than I remembered telling Sean about.

As of that moment I knew Da would become famous overnight.

'Ruined! Ruined! How could one of my own do this to me?'

'It wasn't me, Da. It was your man from Sligo! He did it for the money.'

'You must have known.'

'Honest, Da, I knew nothin'. Not that anyway.'

And I didn't. When I'd see Brains O'Mahony next I'd give him an earful, tell him to pass it on to the Tottenham scout.

'You can recognise the house from the photo,' raved Da. 'Look, it even gives our address. Those Sunday drivers'll come lookin'. It'll be pandemonium!'

I could imagine it already. Hordes of Sunday drivers with cameras trying to get a glimpse of Da.

'That's where he lives.'

'There?'

'Yeah. The biggest dosser in Ireland.'

It took a while for Da to cool down. When he did we all went silent. There wasn't a word spoken for ages.

For a while I thought he might throw me out of the house. Already my mind was working overtime, thinking of where I'd live. Finally, it clicked; I knew of a place. What surprised me was that I'd been thinking all month of where Victor and Henry could stay and couldn't think of anywhere. But when it got to finding a place for myself I thought of one in a few minutes. I suppose that's only natural. When it's you that's in trouble you really get moving.

As it turned out, I needn't have bothered. Da cooled down. But I knew I'd have to take it easy for a while. I was living on borrowed time if I didn't.

Da's starring role in the *Sunday World* was my first surprise of the week. The second happened the following Friday evening, only it wasn't quite as major as the first.

There was a knock on the hall door. I went to answer it. I opened the door – and there were Victor and Henry, newly escaped from Birmingham, standing in front of me. They didn't look too good. They must have visited every dustbin along the way.

Victor had the camcorder with him. They hadn't anything else, only the clothes they stood up in.

Seeing that my family were out, I let them into the house. I gave them a right good feed and a warming at the fire.

They ate practically everything in the fridge (not that there was much due to Da having got there first) before I finally asked, 'What was wrong with Birmingham?'

'There's too many gangs over there. They didn't like us. I think they took exception to Henry's Irish dancing. They didn't like seeing us going around with Terry O'Sullivan neither. Though school was all right and most of the neighbours. It was only the gangs. We couldn't leave Birmingham quick enough … Know where we can stay?'

'Sure. Wait until I go upstairs and get some spare blankets.'

I got the blankets, gave Victor and Henry a good half-hour look at the telly, then got them out of house before anyone came home. I was in enough trouble with my Da as it was.

I took them to where I'd have gone if I'd been kicked out. It was an old house where no one lived, off the Main Street. There was a small yard belonging to the house where a sheep-dog slept in a shed.

There was more. All of which I'll mention another time.

Victor and Henry were home.

Victor, my old mate.

Henry, my outside-right.

Victor and Henry, and us all together again.

It would be as if old times were back.

But would they come back?

Only time would tell.

There are now seven 'Riverside' books

Riverside: The Street-League
Riverside: The Croke Park Conspiracy
Riverside v City Slickers
Riverside: The London Trip
Riverside: Loot!
Riverside: Dynamo Rouge
Riverside: Scout!

PETER REGAN writes from personal experience. He once managed a schoolboy team, and as 'Chick' Regan masterminded the Avon Glens and Brighton Celtic. Today he is a spectator, following the fortunes of Liverpool and Glasgow Celtic.

Born in Keadue in north Roscommon, he now lives in Bray, County Wicklow.

In addition to the 'Riverside' books, he has also written *Urban Heroes*, *Teen Glory* and *Young Champions*. His two fantasy books are *Touchstone* and *Revenge of the Wizards*.